Portia the Pear

by Nicola Hulme

illustrated by Elena Mascolo

WD

TINY TREE
CHILDREN'S BOOKS

First Published 2017
Tiny Tree (an imprint of Matthew James Publishing Ltd)
Unit 46, Goyt Mill
Marple
Stockport
SK6 7HX

www.matthewjamespublishing.com

ISBN: 978-1-910265-xx-x

Illustrations by Elena Mascolo
Printed by Chapel Print
ROCHESTER | www.chapelprint.com

Dedicated to Joy Winkler for her magical inspiration and teachings, also to Leanne, Linda, Jo and "The Wethergirls" for their endless support and encouragement.

Portia pear was a knobbly pear. Her body was twisted. Her skin had dark and pale green patches. Portia longed to be pretty.

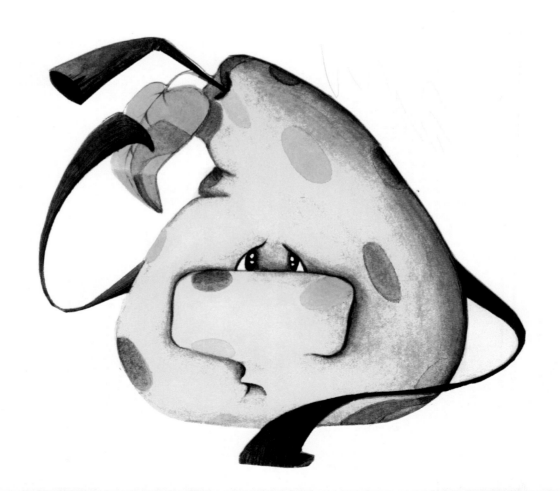

Other pears had beautiful shapes. They
had smooth skin and a lovely green colour.
Some pears had shades of red, which
made them even prettier than the others.

Portia hid herself away
behind the vine leaves, to
hide her crooked shape,

but the gardener kept
pulling the leaves
back to let the sun
warm Portia's skin.

Portia was lonely. She hung
in a space on her own.

Other pears had fruit close to them. Some had made friends and hung in groups of twos or threes.

She could hear them whispering with
their heads close together, and saw
them looking over at her, giggling.

She knew they were making
fun of her twists and bumps
and of her freckled skin.

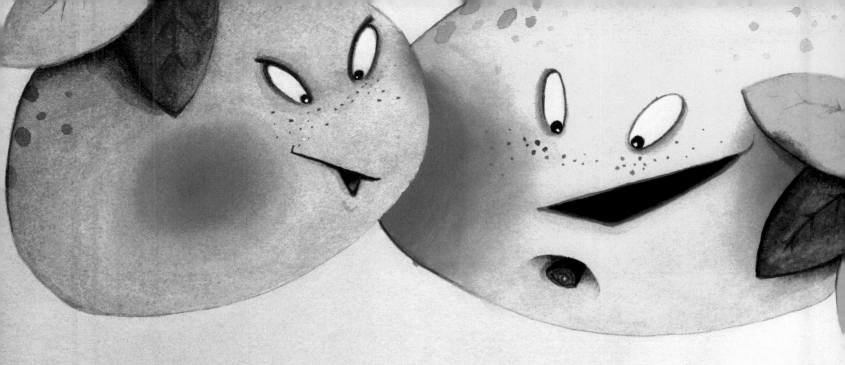

One day, one of them shouted

"I wonder why the gardener doesn't throw her to the compost heap?"

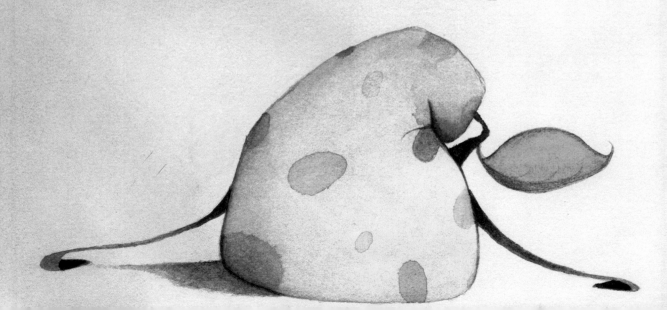

Portia shook behind her leaves, trying to hold back her tears.

"Don't listen to those rotten fruit" said a gentle voice. It was a beautiful butterfly.

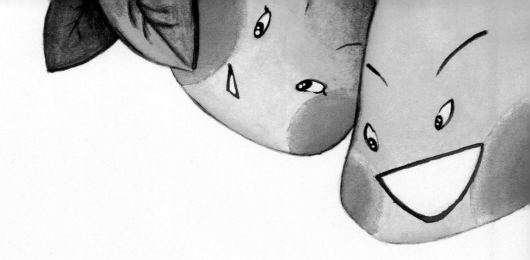

"Every fruit has its place here.
Those two are very naughty
to upset you."

Portia smiled shyly.
Nobody had ever been
kind to her before.

The wind rustled
through the leaves of
a nearby oak tree.

"This will pass"
it whispered
"this will pass."

Portia hoped the tree was right.

She turned her face to the sun for warmth.

As she did, she felt
the vine shake.
There was a pause.

Then it shook again.

This time it shook so hard
she thought she would
fall from the vine.

Then she heard a strange sound;

"Must eat, so hungry, oh my tummy;
must eat, so hungry, oh my tum."

There was a low growling sound
and suddenly a wriggly caterpillar
appeared through the leaves.

"Aha! Lunch" he said as he laid his greedy eyes upon Portia.

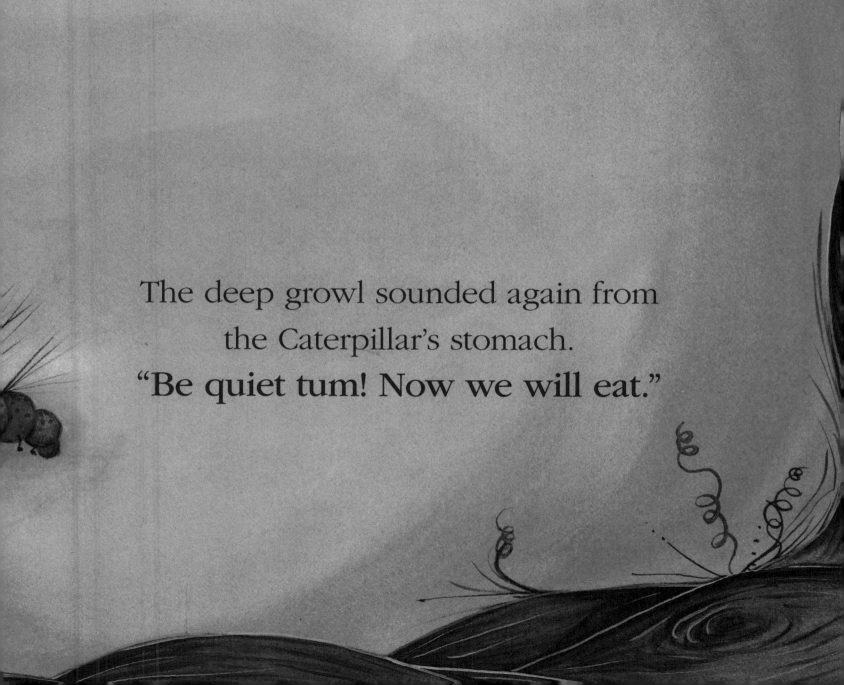

The deep growl sounded again from
the Caterpillar's stomach.
"Be quiet tum! Now we will eat."

Portia tried to think of
a way to escape as the
caterpillar crawled nearer.

He opened his
mouth wide.
Just as he was
about to chomp,
he spotted the plump
pears who hung together
beyond Portia.

"Even better!" the Caterpillar said and off he crawled to make a meal out of the others.

The wind blew through
the great oak.

"This will pass,"
whispered the leaves
"this will pass."

"**Good!**" said a big juicy pear, when the
caterpillar had gone.
"**Those pears were silly. Now I have
more sunlight and I am the best
pear in the garden.**"

Days passed quietly.
The butterfly visited
Portia each day and
sometimes a chirpy
red robin would sit by
her, resting his wings.

He was shy too,
but he smiled
and came
more often
as the days
went by.

It wasn't quiet for long. The handsome pear began to tell everyone in the garden, how he was the best fruit.

He was busy talking, one day, when the wind
blew through the old oak tree.

"This will pass,"
the leaves
whispered
"this will pass."

Five podgy, white fingers
wrapped tightly around the
handsome pear. They squeezed
and tugged him until he
snapped off the vine.

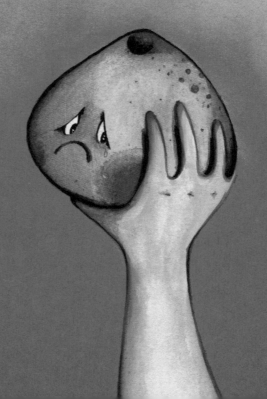

The Park Keeper's daughter had
sneaked into the kitchen garden and
was filling her pockets as she went.

She turned and reached
for Portia, but the Park
Keeper arrived and said,

"There you are, pumpkin. Time to go."

Robin and butterfly
flew to Portia's side
and sat with her
until the little girl
had gone.

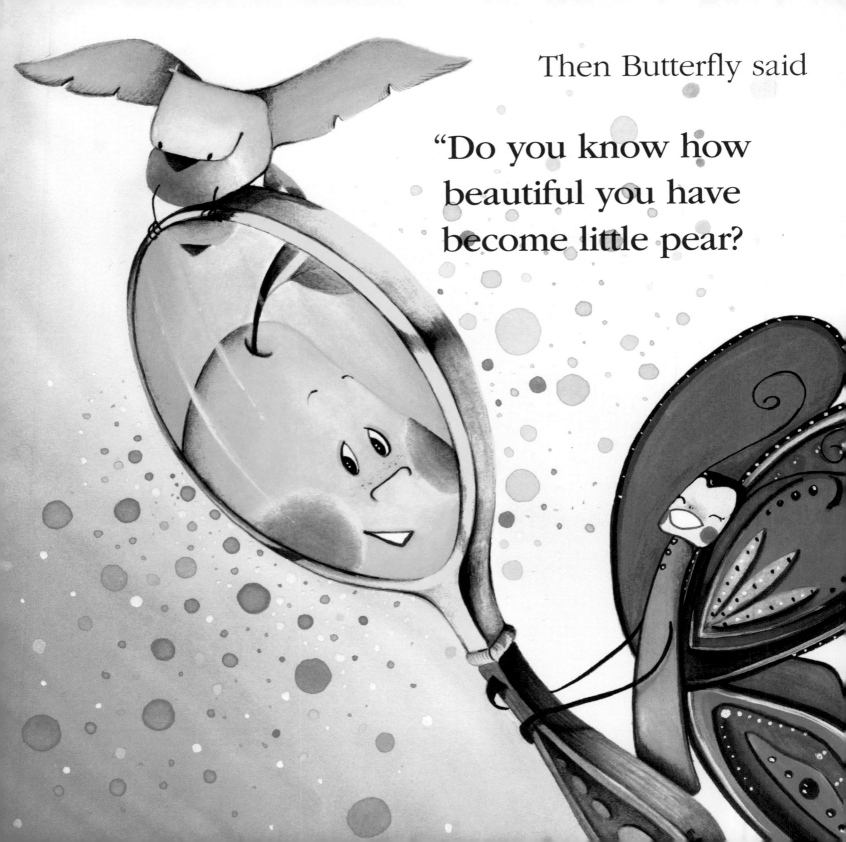

Then Butterfly said

"Do you know how beautiful you have become little pear?

The days in the sun have coloured your skin. You've grown and your wrinkles have gone. You are the prettiest pear now."

"Maybe" said Portia
"but as tree says, this too will pass."

The three friends; robin, butterfly and Portia
sat quietly together. They were glad they were
friends and were sure they would be for a very
long time, no matter how they looked.